105051486   Animal homes

P9-CRK-887

Crabapples

Animal Homes

Tammy Everts & Bobbie Kalman

Crabtree Publishing Company

McLean County Unit #5
Carlock IMC - 105

Crabapples

created by Bobbie Kalman

for Tara, my wonderful sister

Editor-in-Chief
Bobbie Kalman

Writing team
Tammy Everts
Bobbie Kalman

Managing editor
Lynda Hale

Editors
Petrina Gentile
David Schimpky
Janine Schaub

Computer design
Lynda Hale
David Schimpky

Separations and film
Dot 'n Line Image Inc.

Printer
Worzalla Publishing Company

Illustrations
Barb Bedell: pages 8, 13, 14, 18, 22, 23, 30
Antoinette "Cookie" DeBiasi: pages 26-27
Jeannette McNaughton: pages 6, 10, 15, 19, 21

Photographs
Bill Beatty/Visuals Unlimited: page 21
Ernest Braun: page 4 (bottom)
Larry Brock/Tom Stack & Associates: page 4 (top)
John Cancalosi/Tom Stack & Associates: pages 12, 13, 24, 25 (top)
Richard L. Carleton/Visuals Unlimited: page 22
Patrick H. Davies: page 17 (top)
David Edwards/GeoStock: page 11 (bottom)
Joseph L. Fontenot/Visuals Unlimited: page 23
John Gerlach/Visuals Unlimited: pages 5 (bottom), 28 (top)
Victoria Hurst/Tom Stack & Associates: page 5 (top)
James Kamstra: page 30
Larry Lipsky/Tom Stack & Associates: title page, page 28 (bottom)
Diane Payton Majumdar: page 17 (bottom)
Jim Merli/Visuals Unlimited: page 18
Mark Newman/Tom Stack & Associates: page 20
Rod Planck/Tom Stack & Associates: page 16
Dave Taylor: pages 7 (both), 8, 9 (top), 11 (top)
Will Troyer/Visuals Unlimited: page 9 (bottom)
Tom J. Ulrich/Visuals Unlimited: page 14
R. Williamson, BES/Visuals Unlimited: page 25 (bottom)
Robert Winslow/Tom Stack & Associates: cover, page 29

Crabtree Publishing Company

350 Fifth Avenue	360 York Road, RR 4	73 Lime Walk
Suite 3308	Niagara-on-the-Lake	Headington
New York	Ontario, Canada	Oxford OX3 7AD
N.Y. 10118	L0S 1J0	United Kingdom

Copyright © **1994 CRABTREE PUBLISHING COMPANY**. All rights reserved. No part of this publication may be reproduced, stored in a retrieval system or be transmitted in any form or by any means, electronic, mechanical, photocopying, recording, or otherwise, without the prior written permission of Crabtree Publishing Company.

Cataloging in Publication Data
Everts, Tammy, 1970-
  Animal homes

(Crabapples)
Includes index.

ISBN 0-86505-616-1 (library bound)   ISBN 0-86505-716-8 (pbk.)
This book looks at different animal homes, including burrows, webs, nests, and dens.

1. Animals - Habitations - Juvenile literature. I. Kalman, Bobbie, 1947-   . II. Title. III. Series: Kalman, Bobbie, 1947-   . Crabapples.

QL756.E84 1994   j591.56'4   LC 94-22903
                                                              CIP

What is in this book?

A safe place

Some animals roam around and sleep out in the open, but many have homes.

Homes shelter animals from the weather and protect them from their enemies. They provide a safe place for raising babies. Animals also store food in their home.

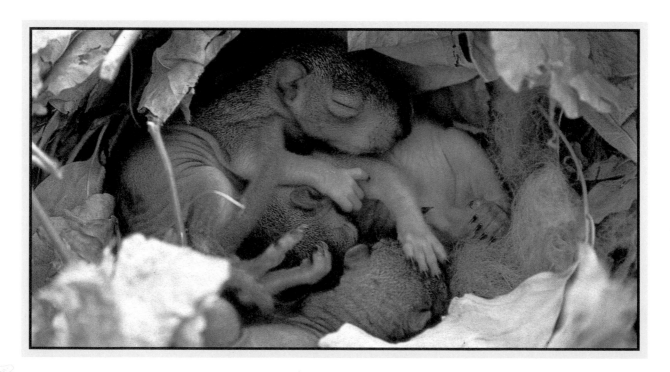

Some animals live alone.
Others live together in groups.
Some animals build their
home. Animals with shells
carry their home with them.

How do animals learn to
build homes? No one really
knows for sure. Experts say
that animals are born knowing
how to do certain things.
This kind of knowledge
is called **instinct**.

A beaver lodge

A beaver's home is called a **lodge**.
Beavers build lodges on rivers or lakes.
They build them away from the shore
and away from their enemies.

A beaver needs deep water to build its lodge. If the water is shallow, the beaver makes a **dam**. A dam is a large pile of wood and stones that is built across a river. It stops water from flowing. The area behind the dam becomes a deep pond.

The beaver uses its sharp front teeth to cut down trees and branches. It pushes the branches across the water to the place where it is building its home. The beaver makes strong walls by packing mud and branches together. It leaves a small hole in the roof for air to enter.

The only way to get into the beaver lodge is through an underwater tunnel. An extra tunnel, which is also under the water, allows the beaver to escape if an enemy enters.

A weaverbird's nest

Have you ever seen a weaver at work? The weaverbird weaves its home in a similar way. A male weaverbird practices weaving when he is a young bird. By the time he is ready to have a family, he is an expert weaver.

The weaverbird uses grass
to build his nest. He weaves
a hanging hoop with his beak
and feet. He sits inside the
hoop and weaves a hollow
ball around himself.

When the nest is finished,
the weaverbird leaves an
opening at the bottom.
He hangs upside down
beneath the nest. He flaps
his wings and sings to attract
a female weaverbird.

If a female likes the nest,
she lines it with soft grass
and moves in. If she does
not like it, the male picks
the nest apart and starts
all over again!

Sometimes many weaverbirds
build nests in the same tree.
The tiny hanging nests look
just like fruit!

A prairie dog town

Dozens of prairie dogs live together in an underground home. They dig long, winding tunnels. The tunnels connect many larger areas that are used as bedrooms, nurseries, and toilets. A prairie dog burrow can be as deep as the basement of a house.

No matter how cold the weather is above the ground, the prairie dog's deep burrow is always warm. A mound of dirt around the opening of the burrow stops rain from entering the home. It also keeps out snow.

Prairie dogs cooperate and look out for one another. During the day, they take turns standing guard on a hill near the burrow. The guard is called a **sentry**.

If the sentry spots an enemy, such as a hawk or a fox, it barks out an alarm. When the other prairie dogs hear the bark, they run to safety beneath the ground. Each burrow has many entrances, so a prairie dog can always escape and hide in a nearby hole.

A fowl nest

The mallee fowl lives in the forests of Australia. This chicken-like bird builds a huge ring-shaped nest on the ground. During the rainy season, the male digs a large pit and fills it with dead plants. When the plants become wet with rain, the mallee fowl covers them with sand.

The wet plants beneath the sand soon begin to rot, or **decompose**. As they decompose, they get warm. When the nest is warm enough, the female mallee fowl digs down and lays her eggs in it.

The nest must stay warm while the young birds are growing inside the eggs. The male mallee fowl checks the temperature with his tongue. If the eggs get too cool, the parents add sand. If the eggs become too hot, the parents take away sand.

Desert tortoise tunnels

The desert tortoise spends most of its life underground. It lives in areas where the summers are hot and dry. In the summer the desert tortoise likes to live alone. It digs a shallow den just big enough to fit inside.

In the winter, the desert tortoise prefers to cuddle up with other tortoises. The tortoises dig a very long tunnel into the slope of a hill. They make a large room, or **chamber**, at the end.

As many as twelve desert tortoises may live in this chamber. In their cosy underground burrow, the tortoises are protected from the freezing winter temperatures.

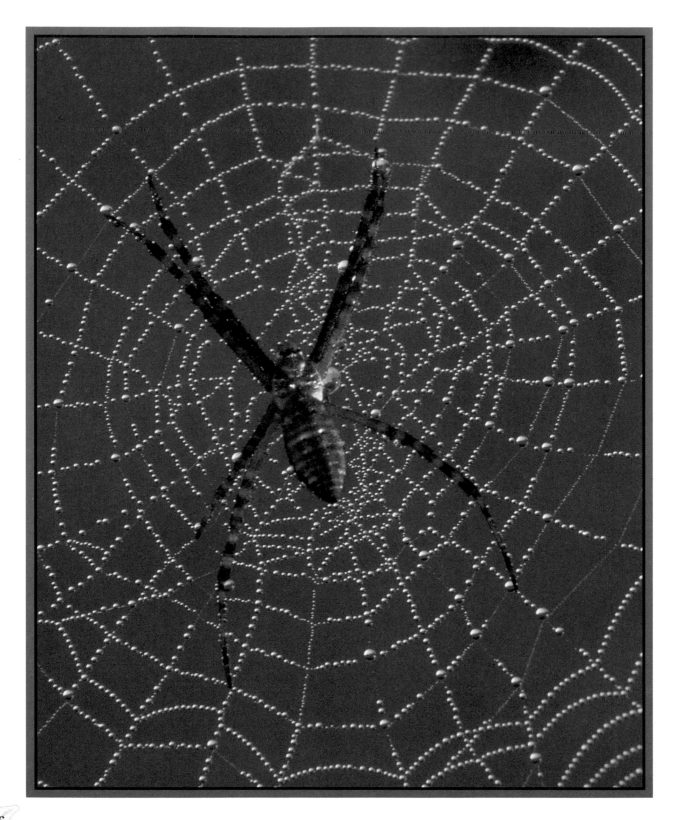

A spider web

A web is both a spider's home and a trap for catching insects. The spider makes its web from a silky thread that it pushes out through the back of its body.

A web can have many shapes. The argiope spider on the opposite page spins a flat web. The trapnet spider, shown top right, makes a bowl-like web. The funnel-web spider's web in the bottom photograph looks like a messy clump of white fluff.

When an insect gets caught in a sticky web, the spider wraps it in silk. The spider kills the insect, unwraps it, and sucks out its juices. It then eats the torn web and spins a new one.

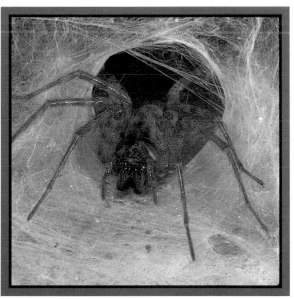

A rabbit warren

Sometimes dozens of rabbits live in communities called **warrens**. A warren is like an underground apartment building.

Rabbits dig several tunnels that are connected to small rooms. The female rabbits do most of the work. They dig with their sharp front claws and kick the dirt out of the tunnel with their strong back legs.

A mother rabbit digs a separate burrow for her babies. She lines the burrow with dry grass and fur from her coat to make it snug and warm. When she leaves to get food, she covers the burrow with leaves and grass.

A **bolthole** is a shallow tunnel that rabbits use to hide from dangerous animals. It is not a home.

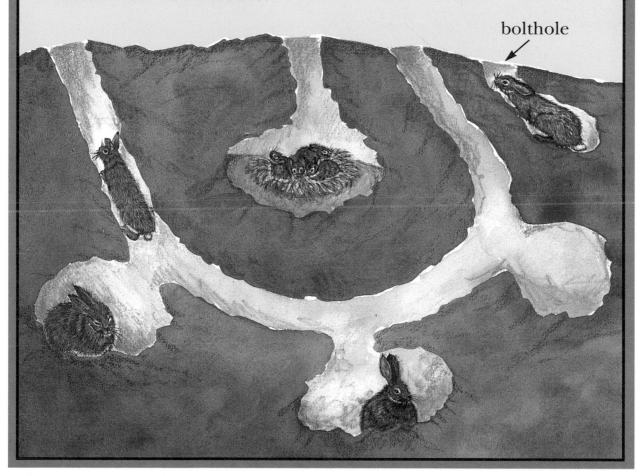

bolthole

Termitaries

Termites are small insects that look like white ants. Most live in hot, dry parts of the world. Some types of termites live in colonies. They build huge homes called **termitaries**. Termitaries can be taller than a one-story building!

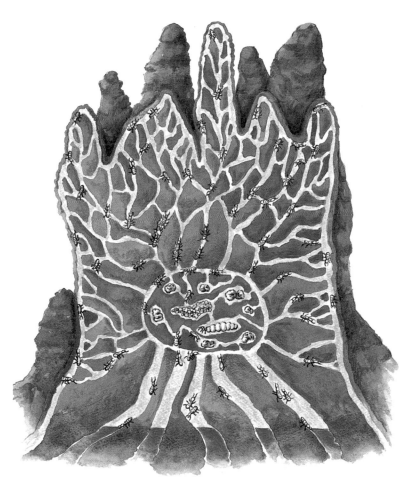

Termites use a mixture of saliva and earth to build hills and towers. Once the walls are dry, they are so hard that they can only be broken with an ax!

The termitary is a maze of tunnels and rooms. There are rooms for storing food, raising young, and growing a **fungus** that termites like to eat. Some termitaries have deep tunnels that provide water!

A crayfish chimney

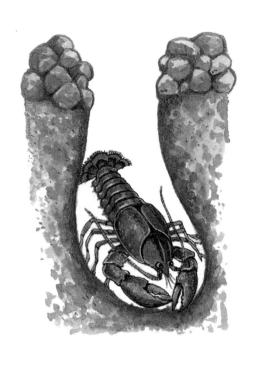

Crayfish are hard-shelled animals that live in wet areas. They look like tiny lobsters. Crayfish need to keep their bodies wet. When the summer heat dries up wet areas, crayfish must look for water under the ground.

A crayfish digs a tunnel with its powerful front claws and pushes the mud out of the hole. The mud dries around the opening. As the tunnel gets deeper, the pile of mud around the entrance grows.

The tall chimney of mud hardens in the hot sun, and the crayfish cannot get out. It sleeps while it is underground. When the autumn rain softens the chimney, the crayfish climbs out. Female crayfish come out with babies clinging to their legs!

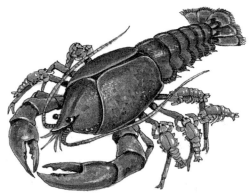

Busy beehive

Honeybees live in large groups called **colonies**. A colony builds a home called a **hive**. The hive is usually located in a shady spot such as the inside of a hollow tree.

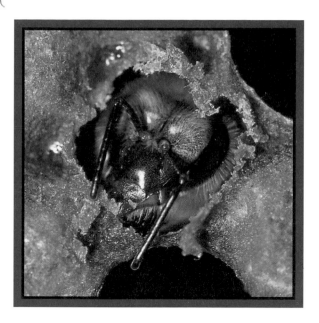

The queen starts the colony. When she is ready to lay eggs, her body produces wax. She uses the wax to build a few small six-sided rooms called **cells**. She lays an egg in each cell. The eggs hatch into smaller worker bees. All the worker bees are female.

The workers build new cells. The queen lays more eggs in these cells. Eventually, the colony has thousands of workers. They collect food and care for the queen bee.

The tailorbird sews a nest

Female tailorbirds build beautiful nests that blend perfectly into the environment. The tailorbird chooses one or two leaves that are still attached to a tree and pulls the edges together with her beak and feet. She uses her sharp beak to poke tiny holes along the sides of the leaves.

After the holes are made, the tailorbird sews the leaves together. She makes her own thread from bark, spider webs, and pieces of plants. She pushes the thread through the holes and ties knots with her beak! When the nest is finished, the tailorbird lines her new home with grass and other soft materials. She is now ready to lay her eggs in her safe nest.

Used homes

Holing up

Many animals do not need to build homes. They simply move into homes that other animals have left behind! Squirrels and chipmunks sometimes take over old woodpecker holes high in trees. These holes are good places to store food and raise families.

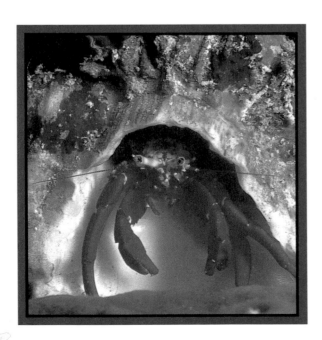

"Shell" I move in?

Hermit crabs do not have a shell to protect their soft bodies, so they move into the empty shells of other creatures! When a hermit crab finds a shell, it tries it on for size. If the shell does not fit, the crab continues its search. If the shell fits, the crab stays inside.

A den of foxes

Each fall, fox families go house-hunting. They look for an empty burrow or hollow log. The den shelters the family during the bitter cold winter. The mother fox cares for the babies, and the father fox brings food to the family. In the spring, the foxes leave their home, and each family member goes its own way.

Pitching a tent

The tent caterpillar gets its name from the tent it builds as a home. Dozens of tent caterpillars work together to build a home among the branches of a tree. The home is made of silky thread that the tent caterpillar produces inside its body. The inside of the tent is safe from birds and other predators.

Words to know

bolthole A shallow tunnel that rabbits use to hide from enemies

chamber A large room

colony A group of insects or animals that live together

dam A pile of wood or stones used to hold back water

decompose To rot

environment The area in which something lives

fowl A bird that is similar to a chicken, turkey, or duck

fungus A mushroom-like plant

instinct A knowledge of how to do things without being taught

lodge A beaver's home

predator An animal that hunts another animal

warren A rabbit's home

termitary A termite mound

Index

What is in the picture?

Here is more information about the photographs in this book.

page:

cover — Red foxes live in the woodlands of the United States and Canada.

title page — Hermit crabs can be found in most of the world's coastal areas.

4 (top) — The least chipmunk lives in North American forests.

4 (bottom) — Baby squirrels are born in soft nests of leaves and grass.

5 (top) — Young red foxes spend the winter in a cosy den.

5 (bottom) — If an enemy comes near a tortoise, it tucks its arms, legs, and head inside its shell.

7 (top) — Beavers live in ponds and rivers throughout North America.

7 (bottom) — A beaver can swim underwater for several minutes before it needs to take a breath.

8 — This picture shows a weaverbird beside its nest. Weaverbirds build their nests close to villages in Africa.

9 (top) — The male weaverbird has a noisy, chattering song.

9 (bottom) — In a weaverbird colony, there are always more females than males.

11 (top) — Prairie dogs live on the plains of North America.

11 (bottom) — Prairie dogs "kiss" as a sign of friendship.

12 — The mallee fowl makes its nest in groves of eucalyptus trees.

13 — Mallee fowl parents work on their nest 24 hours a day.

14 — Desert tortoises live in the deserts of Mexico and the southwestern United States.

page:

16 — Argiope spiders are common in the United States and Canada.

17 (top) — The trapnet spider can be found in many parts of North America.

17 (bottom) — Though Australian funnel-web spiders are poisonous, North American funnel-web spiders like this one are harmless.

18 — European rabbits also live in north Africa, Australia, and even parts of South America.

20, 21 — This termite mound was photographed in Australia, but termites can be found in warm areas around the world.

22 — Crayfish catch their food at night. They eat snails, insect larvae, worms, and tadpoles.

23 — Crayfish that build chimneys are found in North America.

24 — Bees are found throughout the world, but many people believe they first came from Asia.

25 (top) — Young bees grow inside a cell. This full-grown bee is leaving its cell for the first time.

25 (bottom) — This worker bee is feeding nectar to the larvae. Larvae become bees.

28 (top) — The eastern chipmunk lives in eastern North America.

28 (bottom) — This hermit crab makes its home in a queen conch shell.

29 — A female fox gives birth to two to four babies, called kits.

30 — The eastern tent caterpillar lives in eastern North America. The caterpillars grow into tent moths.

McLean County Unit #5
Carlock IMC - 105

1 2 3 4 5 6 7 8 9 0 Printed in USA 3 2 1 0 9 8 7 6 5 4